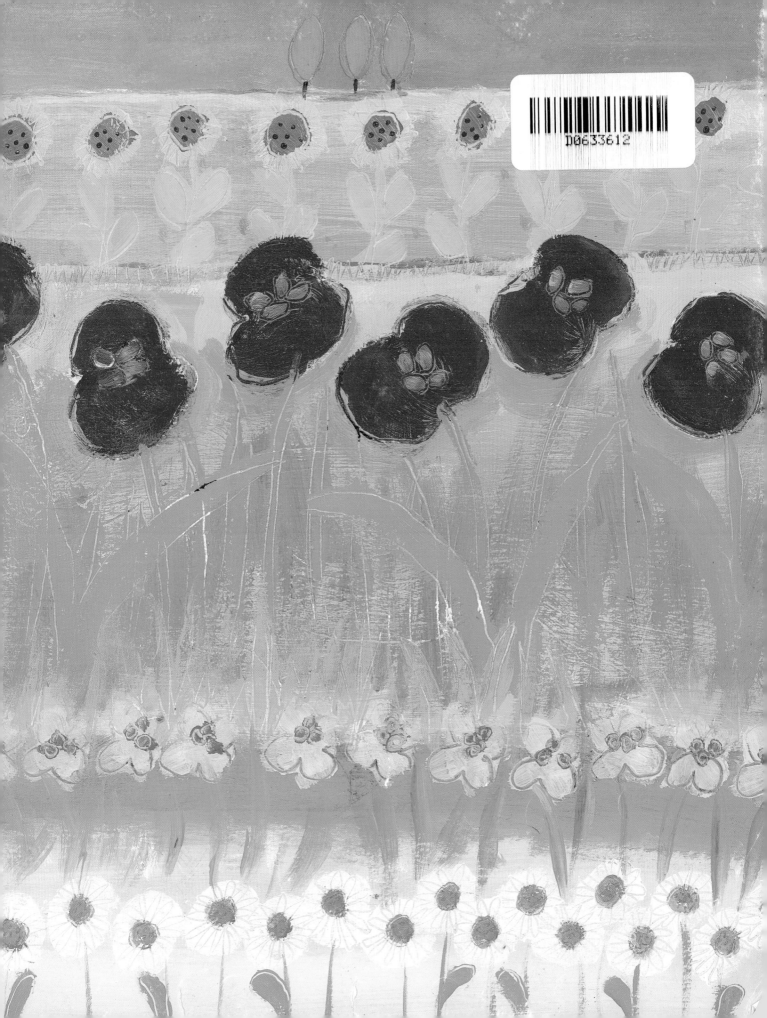

For Tony, Amelia, Alexander, and Theo — J. D-C.

To my auntie, Madeleine — you're a star! — A. B.

First published in 2001 by Macmillan Children's Books
A Division of Macmillan Publishers Limited
25 Eccleston Place, London SW1W 9NF
Basingstoke and Oxford

First U.S. Edition

ISBN: 0-316-60505-0
LCCN 00-111915

10 9 8 7 6 5 4 3 2 1

Printed in Belgium by Proost

Cock-a-Moo-Moo

by Juliet Dallas-Conté

illustrated by Alison Bartlett

LITTLE, BROWN AND COMPANY
BOSTON NEW YORK LONDON

Poor Rooster had forgotten how to crow.

When the sun came up in the morning, he took a deep breath and shouted . . .

"COCK-A-MOO-MOO!"

"That's not right!"
said the cows.
"Only cows go moo."

So he tried again.

"COCK-A-

QUACK-QUACK!"

"That's not right!" said the ducks.
"Only ducks go quack."

So he tried again.

"COCK-A-BAA-BAA!"

"That's not right!" said the sheep.
"Only sheep go baa."

"Silly Rooster!"
said the chickens.
"You're getting it all wrong."

Rooster was very unhappy. "I'm never going to crow again," he said.

But that night, when all the animals were asleep, Rooster heard a noise.

Someone was sniffing . . .
and rustling . . . and sneaking
into the henhouse! It was a . . .

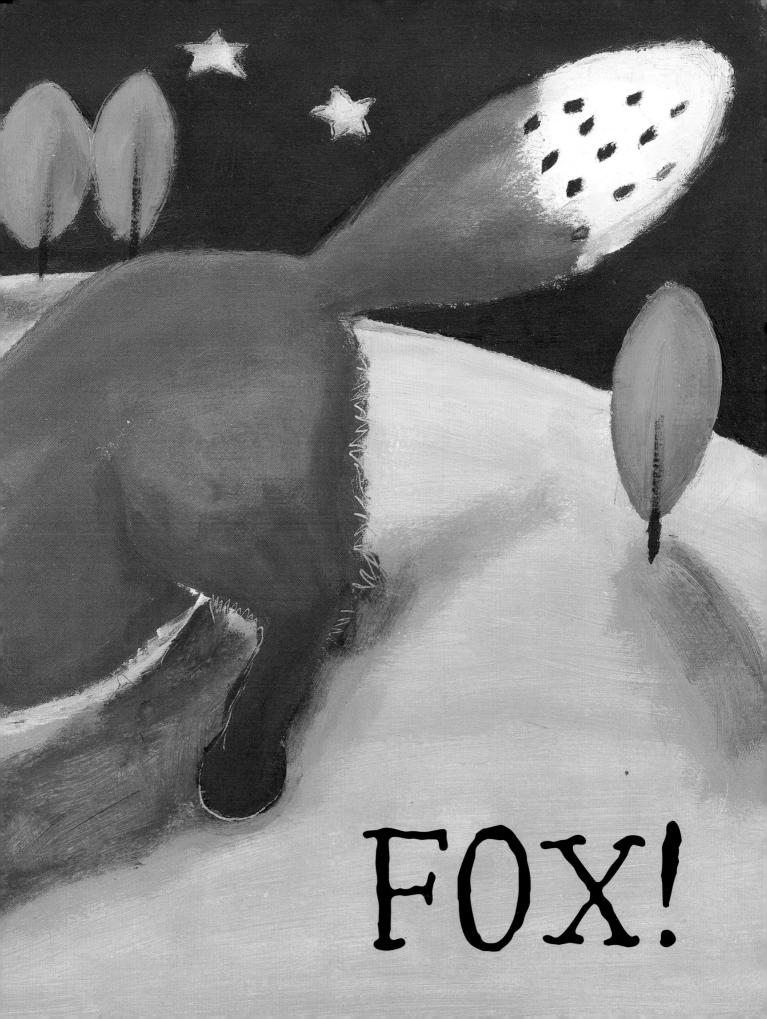

FOX!

"COCK-A-MOO-MOO!" shouted Rooster.

"COCK-A-QUACK-QUACK!

COCK-A-OINK-OINK!

COCK-A-BAA-BAA!"

All the animals woke up!

They came running and
chased the fox away.

"We're saved," clucked the chickens.
"You're a hero!" cried all the animals.
Rooster was so happy.

"COCK-A-
DOODLE-
DOO!"

he crowed.

And he never got it wrong again.

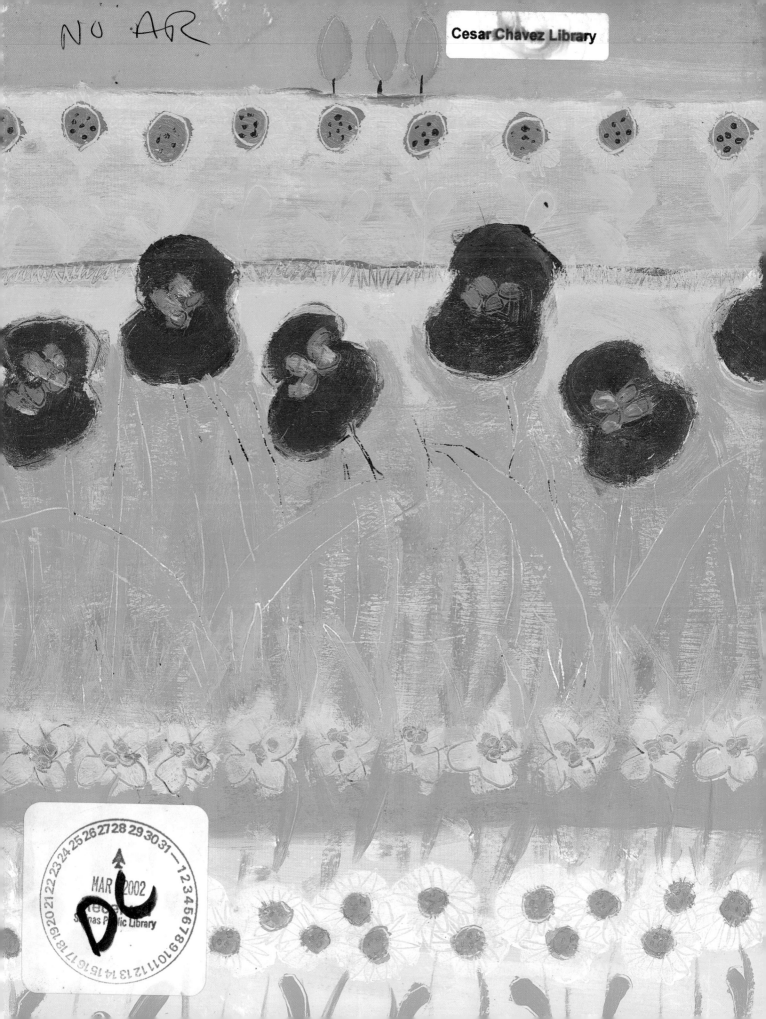